THE TRUE STORY OF A YOUNG HEROINE AND A LIGHTHOUSE

Abbie Against The Storm

Written by *Marcia Vaughan*

Illustrated by *Bill Farnsworth*

BEYOND
WORDS
Publishing
I N C

Beyond Words Publishing, Inc.
20827 N.W. Cornell Road, Suite 500
Hillsboro, Oregon 97124-9808
503-531-8700 / 1-800-284-9673

Edited by Marianne Monson-Burton
Designed by Andrea Boven

Distributed to the book trade by Publishers Group West
Printed in Italy

Library of Congress Cataloging-in-Publication Data

Vaughan, Marcia K.
Abbie against the storm: the true story of a young heroine and a lighthouse
/ written by Marcia Vaughan; illustrated by Bill Farnsworth

Summary: A fictionalized account of an incident in the life of a seventeen-year-old girl
who tends her family's lighthouse during a fierce storm on the coast of Maine in the winter of 1856.

ISBN 1-58270-007-9
1. Burgess, Abbie, 1839-1892 Juvenile fiction.
[1. Burgess, Abbie, 1839-1892 Fiction. 2. Lighthouse keepers Fiction.]
I. Farnsworth, Bill, ill. II. Title.
PZ7.V452Ab 1999 [E]–dc21

99-25496
CIP

The corporate mission of Beyond Words Publishing, Inc: *Inspire To Integrity*

Abbie
Against
The
Storm

For my mom and dad,
Helen and Claude Pearson, with love —MARCIA

For my wife, Deborah
and our daughters, Allison and Caitlin —BILL

A BRINY BREEZE
tugged playfully at Abbie's hair as waves
washed like soapy water over her bare feet.
She glanced over her shoulder at the
guardian lighthouse towers. They rose
up from the jumble of sea-swept stones
called Mantinicus Rock.

*A*BBIE'S FATHER HAD COME TO the Rock to keep the lighthouse. "It's not a grand place, but it's important, to be sure," he told his family on the morning they arrived. "The light from the towers is the only signal to keep ships from running aground on the rocks. Without it burning bright every night, there'd be a fearful loss of lives."

In the days that followed, Abbie's sisters found the island to be a treasure-trove of animals and sea creatures. Unlike Esther, Mahala, and Lydia, Abbie was curious about the working of the lighthouse. While her sisters played hide-and-seek amid the rocks, Abbie helped her father organize the barrels of whale oil, clean the tower windows, and make entries in the leather-bound logbook.

"Don't most lighthouse keepers have assistants?" she asked her father, as their shadows danced up the narrow stairway.

"Some do, some don't," he replied. "Why do you ask?"

Abbie stood up straight. "I could be your assistant," she said, hopefully.

As they reached the top, Papa kissed her forehead. "Abbie, my girl, you already are."

When the sun set, Abbie and Papa watched their beacon cast a shimmering path across the water. Abbie imagined what relief a sailor would feel seeing their light shine through the pitch-dark night.

"The last lighthouse keeper told me waves sweep clear across the island during winter storms," her father mentioned.

Abbie shuddered at the thought. "Do you think it's true?"

"We'll find out soon enough," he replied.

*P*APA SHOWED ABBIE HOW TO carefully clean the twenty-eight Argand lamps. Side by side, they polished the silver reflectors behind each lantern. "Any smudge or speck of dirt will darken the lens," Papa said.
So Abbie polished the metal until she could see her reflection smiling back. "You're doing a fine job, Abbie," Papa told her. She couldn't help but smile.

Abbie gazed across the sea and thought of her older brother. "Do you think Ben's fishing boat is out there, Papa?"

"It could well be," he nodded. "As long as the ships can see our light, they'll sail safe upon the deep, dark sea. But Abbie, if the lights were to fail, even for a short time, a ship could be dashed to pieces on the rocks and all hands lost."

SUMMER PASSED AWAY LIKE A golden dream. In September the supply ship didn't come. As the air turned chill, Papa began to worry. Their store of dried beef, flour, salt pork, and beans was nearly gone, and Mother's coughing grew worse.

"I can wait no longer, my girl," Abbie's father said on a gray day in January. "I must sail for Rockland at first light."

Worry stirred in Abbie's stomach. "Who will mind the lights?"

Papa rested his hand on Abbie's shoulder. "You know as much about these lights as I do. You'll do as fine a job as any lighthouse keeper, of that I'm sure. Don't worry, Abbie. I'll only be gone overnight."

But Abbie did worry. She'd never taken care of the lights alone.

At sunrise Papa climbed into the family's dory. The icy waves sighed and whispered around Abbie's ankles as she pushed against the bow. The boat scraped over the rocks and into the restless sea.

"Keep the lights shining bright, my girl," Papa called, hoisting the canvas sail.

"I will," Abbie answered, trying to sound more confident than she felt.

Papa waved. A stiff morning breeze filled the sail, and the boat skimmed across the water toward Rockland, twenty miles away.

*A*BBIE'S FEET POUNDED ON THE stairs as she raced up the tower. She pressed her face to the window, watching Papa's boat disappear.

Suddenly Abbie felt overwhelmed at the thought of keeping the lights by herself. Panic washed over her like a cold wave. *What if I fail?*

She pushed the worry away as she cleaned the lamps until every speck of dust was removed. Abbie was pulling the canvas hood over them when she heard the wind pick up.

Within an hour, dark clouds blocked the sun and a bitter wind bullied the waves, blowing swirls of spray off the white caps. Abbie looked out across the Atlantic thinking of Papa in the small dory.

WITH EACH PASSING HOUR THE wind increased. By evening, rain drummed heavily on the roof and the thunder of the surf was so loud that Abbie had to raise her voice to be heard. "It's getting dark early," she said. "I'm going to light the lamps."

"I'm coming, too," said Mahala.

Abbie's hands were shaking as she struck a match and held it over the wick. *What if the oil's too cold? What if the wick won't light?* The match flickered and died as terror gripped her.

"Hurry, Abbie!" whispered Mahala.

She took another match from the box. *Light the lamps, Abbie. You know how to do this.* She willed her fingers to be steady as she struck a second match. The flame died down, flickered, then flashed to life. The wick glowed red.

Abbie let out a long sigh. Finally her hands found their rhythm. One by one she lit the lamps until a bright white beacon of light punched a hole through the rising storm.

$\mathscr{A}$LL NIGHT ABBIE STAYED WITH the lights. By morning, the storm was whipping the water into mountainous waves that surged over the edge of the island.

Hurrying down the stairs, she gasped at the sight of sea water swirling under the front door, flooding the floor. The wind was reaching gale-force, so she secured the shutters and put extra blankets on Mama's bed.

"I've got to bring the hens in," Abbie told her mother, "before they wash away!"

Mama looked paler than the day before. "That wind is fierce, Abbie. You'd best wear your father's old oilskin slicker."

Lydia pulled on her arm. "Don't go, Abbie. The waves are so big they'll wash you away!"

"I've got to save the hens. Stay with Mama and close the door tight behind me." Wrapped in the slicker, Abbie grabbed the basket and stepped out into the fury of the storm.

*I*T WAS WORSE THAN SHE THOUGHT. The ocean bucked and heaved like a wild horse. The raw wind ripped the roof from the oil shed, shattering shingles against the rocks. Abbie staggered on, waiting for one roller to recede before stepping forward. She made a run for the hen house. Waves pulled at her feet and swirled around her knees, moving the rocks beneath her. Her soggy skirts dragged.

Unlatching the door, she scooped the frightened hens into the basket, covering them with a blanket. Bending her head against the gale, she clutched the basket tightly in her arms and battled back toward the house.

Abbie dashed inside shivering, and Lydia peeked inside the basket. "You saved them all!"

Mama stroked Abbie's cold, wet cheek. "I'm proud of you, Abbie. We'll need the eggs to keep us fed till Papa returns."

"Look what's coming!" Esther exclaimed as the sea rose up like a giant's hand. *"Close the door!"* cried Mama. The first monstrous wave took the oil shed, the second swept away the fog bell. The next slapped the hen house off its foundation, as boards and shingles were swallowed up by the raging sea.

The sea rose again, hammering against the house like a fist, knocking pictures from the wall and books from the shelves. Suddenly, the sound of splintering glass echoed from above.

"*T*HE LIGHTS!" SCREAMED ABBIE. Fear pounded in her heart as she raced up the stairs of the south tower. On the floor lay a pile of shattered glass. "Only a lantern," she said, shaking with relief.

Outside, breakers tore across the island, slamming against the granite walls of the lighthouse. As Abbie paused to replace a picture, the wall trembled and a terrifying thought grew in her mind. *What if the sea should swallow the whole house?*

"The safest place is the north tower," she said to her sisters. "Help me move Mama." Racing against the rising water, they hurried down again and again, grabbing matches, blankets, water jugs, the hens, and the last of the food.

"Hurry!" Abbie cried, but the storm drowned out her voice. They had barely reached the top step when a crash sounded below.

"What's happening down there?" Mama whispered.

CAUTIOUSLY ABBIE CREPT DOWN
the stairs. Her eyes widened with shock. "The sea is everywhere!"
she called.

Mama drew the girls tightly around her. Mahala began to
cry. "I want Papa!"

Mama stroked Mahala's hair. "You know he can't set out to
sea in such a storm. He'll come home as soon as the sea is
calm."

All through the night Abbie worked—warming the oil,
trimming the wicks, filling the reservoirs. Her feet were numb
from wading through the water to reach the south tower.

Outside the gale howled like a wild animal. Mama and the girls
huddled close under the wool blankets, dozing and waking as
waves thundered against the tower.

$\mathcal{A}$BBIE THOUGHT OF THE SHIPS
fighting their way through the rolling sea, trying to avoid
treacherous rocks that thrust like jagged teeth from the
Atlantic. She thought of Ben out there in the storm. *Whatever
you do, Abbie, don't give up. Keep the lights burning!*

Twice Abbie had to go out on the slick catwalk.
Clenching her teeth, she willed herself not to look down at
the ragged waves that surged up the side of the tower.
Clutching desperately to the rail, she scraped off the ice as
quickly as she could and climbed back inside.

At times her eyelids felt so heavy she wanted only to curl
up and sleep. *Will it never end?* she wondered, as exhaustion
threatened to overtake her. But even stronger than Abbie's
desire to sleep was her determination to succeed. Hour after
hour she kept the lights burning bright, and the lighthouse
stood firm against the storm.

*A*S THE FIRST GRAY LIGHT OF dawn finally broke through the turbulent sky, Abbie was filled with a strange feeling. *Even when I'm sleeping I watch the lights. They have become part of me, and I have become part of them.*

Although the worst of the storm had passed, the wind still whipped the waves as hours turned into days and days turned into weeks. Still the churning sea kept Abbie's father from returning.

To keep from starving, the last of the food was rationed. For four long weeks, Abbie, her mother, and three sisters survived on one egg apiece and a cup of cornmeal mush each day.

Not once in all that time did the lights fail. Not one ship floundered. Not one life was lost.

Finally one evening, Abbie spotted a dot on the horizon. "Please," she prayed, "let it be Papa." Slowly the dot became a boat, and as the sun dipped into the sea, Papa landed the dory. Abbie raced down the stairs to greet him.

*H*E CAUGHT HER UP IN HIS ARMS AND hugged her hard. "You did it, Abbie!" he beamed. "Guided by your lights, countless ships sailed safely into Rockland. My girl, it's true. You are the best lighthouse keeper on the coast of Maine!"

Abbie's spirit soared as a feeling of enormous pride glowed within her—pride at being Abbie Burgess and a keeper of the lights.

EPILOGUE

After surviving the worst storm in two hundred years, Abbie helped her father mind the lights on Mantinicus Rock for seven years. When he retired, Abbie stayed to assist the new lighthouse keeper, Mr. Grant. She fell in love with his son, Isaac. After they married in 1861, Isaac and Abbie kept the lights for fourteen years. Their four children were born there. For her work Abbie was paid $440.00 per year.

In 1875 Isaac and Abbie were transferred to the Whitehead Light Station in Maine. After twenty-two years, Abbie said farewell to the Rock. Abbie lived to be fifty-two years old, having spent the last thirty-eight years of her life at lighthouses. Before her death in 1892 she wrote, *"I wonder if the care of the lighthouse will follow my soul after it has left this worn-out body. If I ever have a gravestone, I would like it in the form of a lighthouse."* Fifty-three years later, her wish was granted as a miniature replica of the Mantinicus Rock lighthouse was placed on her grave.